Rabbit's Legend

written by Pam Holden
illustrated by Lamia Aziz

Rabbits are quiet animals that are well-known for their long ears and excellent hearing. But they have not always had such long furry ears. Many years ago, rabbits were quite noisy and had short round ears, until one rascal decided to play a trick on all his friends.

2

One day the rascal Rabbit was feeling bored with nothing to do, so he asked Beaver, "Do you know that the sun isn't ever going to rise again? Today is the last day with sunshine."

4

Beaver was shocked to hear such dreadful news. "It will be like the cold winter all the time!" he cried. "I wonder if Squirrel knows about this."

"Everyone needs to know," said Rabbit, hiding a sly smile behind his paws.

"I must tell Squirrel right now," replied Beaver, as he hurried away.

"This is terrible!" cried Squirrel. "Every animal needs to gather food to store for the cold dark days. I'll tell Raccoon to get ready."

Raccoon told Skunk, who rushed to warn Chipmunk. Soon all the animals were feeling worried as they scampered about collecting extra food for their families. As soon as Mouse was told, he raced to find Bear.

8

When Bear heard the bad news he felt very upset and puzzled.
He told his family to stop playing in the sunshine, and start
eating as many berries and leaves as they could, so they would
grow fat and wouldn't need much more food.

Rabbit chuckled as he watched all the animals rushing around busily, getting ready for those awful days when the sun didn't shine any more. He thought it was funny that one short message from him had caused such a huge fuss.

12

While Rabbit was hiding in the bushes, laughing to himself, Moose came walking along to visit his friends. But none of the animals stopped to talk to him as they usually did. He called out, "Hello, Bear. Hi, Squirrel. How's everything?"

"Sorry, Moose, I haven't time to chat," replied Bear.

"We mustn't stop working today," called Squirrel.

14

Moose felt surprised as he walked further looking for a friend,
but everyone he met seemed too busy to take any notice of him.
Knowing something must be wrong, he asked Beaver, "Why
won't anybody talk to me? Please tell me what's happening."

"Haven't you heard?" Beaver cried. "The sun isn't going to shine any more, so we must get ready for winter now. We need to store such an enormous amount of food! We must hurry because this is the last day of sunshine!"

Moose shook his wide horns in amazement, then called all the
animals together to hear what he wanted to say.
They gathered around in a circle saying, "Tell us quickly.
We must get straight back to work!"
"This story isn't true! There will be plenty more days with
sunshine. Someone has tricked you," Moose explained.
"Whoever told you this silly story, Bear?"
"Mouse told me!" growled Bear. "He said that Chipmunk
warned him."

Chipmunk said, "I heard it from Skunk. Raccoon told him."

"It was Beaver who warned me," said Raccoon. "He
 heard the message from Rabbit."

"But you all know that Rabbit is a rascal! Where is he
now?" asked Moose.

"Wherever is he?" cried all the animals together. "That
wicked rascal must be hiding. We'll find him right now!"

Quickly they hunted among trees, rocks and logs. Bear soon found Rabbit hiding low in thick bushes. He grabbed him by his short round ears and pulled him out of his hiding place, lifting him up high.

The animals felt foolish for believing Rabbit's ridiculous story.
One by one they told him what a nasty trick he had played,
making them work so hard to prepare for cold dark days without
sunshine. Bear kept holding Rabbit up by his ears while every
animal told him how mean he had been.

By the time Rabbit said that he was sorry, something strange had happened to his ears! When Bear put him down, all the animals gasped to see such long ears! They had stretched!

That's how Rabbit changed into a long-eared, quiet animal.
He discovered that his long ears were excellent for listening,
and he learned to never play silly tricks again.